----For my daughter, Xian.

About the Author:

Huaicun Zhang is Tu Ethnic Minority, British Chinese. She is a member of the Chinese Writers' Association and the Royal Society of British Artists. She has held art exhibitions in Hong Kong, Macau, Seoul, Tokyo, New York City, Paris and London.

Publications include: *Pencil Tree, One Snowflake, The Oasis in My Heart, The Red House, On the Train of Autumn, Space of Freedom, Huaicun and Her Friends, Listening to the Flower Bloom, Huaicun's Chinese Painting and Calligraphy.*

Huaicun has translated *My Name is Bob, BBC Nation's Favourite Poetry about Childhood, The Red Tiles, The Sky is The Limit* and other English illustrated books and poetry selections. Her most recent books include: *On the Train of Autumn and The Habitat for Fairy Tales.*

About the Translator:

Ms. Wang Dan, British Chinese, a Legal officer and translator, has been awarded a Master of Biochemical Engineering by University of Birmingham, and a Master of Laws by the University of Law in the United Kingdom. Ms. Wang enjoys reading books in History and Culture. She is also fond of exploring the culture and history of different countries. Her translation works include *The Pencil Tree, The Habitat for Fairy Tales*, and etc. Ms. Wang is currently living in London.

CONTENTS

< 1 >

< 2 >

PENCIL TREE

< 3 >

PENCIL TREE

< 4 >

PENCIL TREE

Huaicun

< 5 >

AS HAPPY AS A CHILD

The Fragrant Olive is flowering in August.
It is a wonderful season that
I illustrate in the studio, while
Birds are singing out of the window.

We argue about the colour and the apple
In the Hungry Caterpillar.
Whether the colour represents its childhood,
And whether the apple is the home for the Caterpillar.

The Chinese Redbuds are blooming,
With bees buzzing in the blossoms.
Birds are jumping joyfully on the branches,
With their chirping wafting in the Fragrant Olives.

At the moment, my heart is full of the lush grassland,
And colourful flowers from all over the hills.
At the moment, you possess
A unique colour, and
A particular fragrance.

< 6 >

PENCIL TREE

< 7 >

CLUSTERS OF FLOWERS

The childhood leaves quietly,
Disappearing behind the garden door.
The sun, the moon, the stars and the clouds
All hide into my diary.

Pigeons on the roof flee.
The kitten in the loft disappears.
With the breeze in the fall whistling,
Everything fades into darkness.

Clifford flowers close their eyes.
Butterflies fall asleep.
In the hay, the bunny is resting.
On the pasture, the pony is dozing.
The puppy lies on the master's sofa.

When the grassland is silent,
The beautiful songs wafting out of the hut
Are sung by Mother who counts the stars
in the moonlight.

< 8 >

PENCIL TREE

The singing never ceases until Granny stops spinning the prayer's
wheel, and Until Father gently turns off the television.

The clouds shortly appear
Brighter and brighter in the east.
On the pillars of the hut creep up the white morning glories.
As soon as the rooster gets up, it starts crowing.

The grass, the breeze, the birds, the crickets,
The houses, the forest and the spiders…
Opening their eyes and stretching their bodies,
They all hear the clip-clop of the horses passing by.

The girl, holding the painting brush in her hand and dreaming, is
awakened.
The sun rushes through her door;
Her room is turned into red by the glow, and
Her drawing paper is moistened by the dew.

The dreaming girl is awake,
Rolling on the fluffy felt.
The painting brush in her hand fills her in colours,
Just like clusters of flowers in spring.

< 9 >

Huaicun

She is like the Flower Child in last night's TV show,
Like the chipmunk in Black Cat Detective,
Like the youngest boy in Calabash Brothers,
And like Sneezy in Snow White.

Every movement and each smile
Will become a fairy tale in the hut.
The roses in the garden
Are all grinning to her.

< 10 >

THE PENCIL TREE

The coloured pencils
Are my favourite.
But I accidentally lost them.

I had a dream at night,
In which the river,
The field,
And the forest
Were all colourful.

The grass appeared,
Waving its hand to me.
So did the stars,
Blinking at me.

They all spoke to me loudly:
We are drawn
by the coloured pencils.

The pencil trees were everywhere
And colourful.
They were dancing happily
On the drawing paper.

During the jumping and dancing,
A flower came out,
Nodding at me.

< 11 >

I AM ON THE MOON.

Sitting on the crooked moon,
I am whispering with the stars.
Casted by its velvety light,
I am reading on the moon.

The sparkling stars
And the gentle moon
Are embracing me firmly.

The moon seems to be a lamp,
While I am painting on it.

< 12 >

SWAYING

The star comes to my bed,
With its eyes blinking.

The kitten sprawls on my blanket,
With its whiskers moving.

The bunny lies under my bed,
With its ears trembling.

My little doll
Is staying in my arms quietly.

Mum's voices
Are wafting to my ears
From the study.

Swaying, gently swaying.

< 13 >

LIQUOR IN THE SPRING

The rain comes
In the morning
In their shining costume.
It happily falls,
Fascinating the spring.
Mum tells me that it is liquor in the spring.

< 14 >

IN THE EYES OF A CHILD

The net in Grandpa's hand is
Too fine and too dense,
Too big and too small, and
Too short and too long
To fish up the dreams.
The world is full of laughter
And fairy tales.
The laughter will sprout in the spring drizzle.
The fairy tales will grow up in the autumn mizzle.
All of them will become immature fruits
As well as fantastic hopes.

< 15 >

HAPPINESS IS FLOURISHING.

My heart is
A tiny seed.

In spring,
It hides in the fields,
Waiting for the breeze.

In summer,
It sits in the buttercups,
Whispering to the birds.

In autumn,
It stands by the Lotus pond,
Listening to stories told by the Moon.

In winter,
It turns into a sparkling snowflake,
Dancing in the sun.

Please listen.
The hearts are singing.
The happiness
Is
Flourishing.

< 16 >

FAIRY TALES IN SPRING

It is the cloud
That mirrors the beautiful forests.

It is the thunder
That wakes up the sleeping worms.

It is the drizzle
That asks the lovely flowers to dance.

It is the warbling birds
That tell us to take off the jackets.

They are
All
Talking about
Fairy tales in spring.

< 17 >

SONGS IN SUMMER

The trees sprout,
Wandering around joyfully
With the flowers.
The birds fly into the forest,
Jumping on the grass
In the wind.

The sun is shining on the path.
Beautiful butterflies fly by.
Busy bees buzz off.
Lovely ants creep out.
Delighted us come over.
On the winding path,
The summer
Is approaching,
Singing and painting
Along the road.

There are colours
Ornamenting on each branch in the forest.

< 18 >

PENCIL TREE

Huaicun

< 19 >

THE KOALA BEAR
IN THE PENCIL TREE

The summer is dancing in the poems.
When the sun sets,
A koala bear is climbing up a pencil tree.
The fireflies are frolicking among the pencil trees
with their lanterns.

The moonlights hide under the pencil trees,
Running in the lawn towards the clear lake.
Shall we leave all the happiness
and worries to the sun tomorrow?
Let's be a koala bear in the pencil tree tonight.

Alexander Pushkin is coming
Into the pencil trees
With his Ruslan and Ludmila.
He is singing loudly,
"A green oak by the sea,
On which a learned cat walks back
and forth On a gold chain.
When the cat walks to the right, he sings

< 20 >

PENCIL TREE

To the left he tells stories.
In this magical place,
Fairy tales come alive…"

A koala bear is running among the pencil trees
In the moonlight.

Huaicun

< 21 >

Huaicun

THE SPRING ON THE WAY

Our laughter is everywhere
To decorate the beautiful March.
Poetry is walking quietly in the sun in spring.
We are as exuberant as March in spring.

Why is spring so charming?
The grass flourishes and
Becomes longer, thicker and more beautiful
Just in one day.

< 22 >

PENCIL TREE

All the trees are sprouting.
Birds' chirpings fly over the manor.
Their voices are as beautiful as melody,
Wafting from the trees into the ears.

At the moment, I am full of joys.
Blossoms and leaves of the pear trees are smooth
and shining.
Clouds are floating
on the clear sky that is in a fantastic blue.
Lambs in the fields can't stop frolicking.
What makes me feel delighted?
It must be the spring on the way.

< 23 >

A GOLDEN DAWN

I wake up in a golden dawn,
Feeling the breeze
In the splendour of you and the sun.
I attempt to prolong this fairy tale.

I wish all of them
Would become everlasting stories,
As eternal as the sun, the moon and the stars.

A river is waiting
For a breeze
And a ray of sunlight.
If bending down and listening to the dewdrop,
I will hear a beautiful melody.
When your cordial and soft voice
Wakes me up,
A new fairy tale has been made
In the forest on a sunny day.

< 24 >

Huaicun

< 25 >

THE AUTUMN

The autumn passes my house
To welcome the pleasant winter.
It is running and jumping,
Whom the spring will even try to avoid.

It runs into my studio,
Listening to the rustle of my brush,
Watching my child climbing up the stairs,
And looking at the toys dancing in the hall.
Everything is about the spring.

My dear friends, I have never been so excited.
In my studio,
All the laughter has been left by the autumn.
I have never been so calm,
Peaceful and tranquil.

< 26 >

The house has red walls, green windows and blue roof,

Where the sunlight will settle down, and

Where it will be full of

The children's happy songs

And the wonderful fairy tales.

< 27 >

A LITTLE MOUSE

The mouse is little, fat and white,
Jumping in the fireplace.
It is looking at all the paintings on the table, and
Finds its favourite.

You, the mouse catching my special attention,
Are gnawing on a rice paper
With the sharp teeth.

You, the mouse I always remember,
Are sneaky
And naughty.
You are as furry as a hairball, and
drive away all my tiredness.

< 28 >

THE SPRING

I feel exalted as my desire is increasing.
I am gazing out of the window with joy and find
The spring walking past my house cheerfully.
it makes the birds keep chirping.

I feel exalted as the spring finally comes.
It is stepping into my garden delightedly and
Turning the whole hill to green.
The fragrance of grass can be caught
even far from the sky.

< 29 >

MARCH

March is a time to write poetry,

Please provide us with splendid flowers today.

Each poet has their own memory in March,

Please bring us the happiness hiding in the garden.

Don't allow me to leave with my heart, and

Ask me to stay instead.

In spring, which is the most vigorous season of the year,

There are poems everywhere,

Like the wind in Mobei Grassland,

Like the snow at the foot of Qilian Mountain, and

Like the Yellow River in the dream…

< 30 >

< 31 >

LISTEN, IT IS THE FOOTSTEPS OF THE SPRING.

At six o'clock in the morning,
the birds' chirping awakens me.
The sky seems to glow with a pale light,
Making the dawn as crystal as a dew.
The sun is shining. I feel exalted.
But the misery of missing the hometown and
its flowers is also accompanied.

I am missing and crying from time to time,
Which can be confirmed by the swing in the courtyard.

At the moment, I am sitting on the stone in the garden,
Staying in the morning sun and the mist,
Listening to the spring approaching, and
Missing the hometown smell of horse manure
in the grasslands.

< 32 >

PENCIL TREE

It is a wonderful morning.
The jasmine tree by the watermill has already sprouted,
the scents waft out.
My thoughts are floating around over the pond
in the morning,
Accompanied by the insects on the lawn,
murmuring about the spring.

The fragrance of the soil drifts over my garden
with the wind.
Listen, spring is approaching.
When she comes out of the forest,
the garden bustles with noise immediately.
Listen, it is the footsteps of the spring.

< 33 >

THE MUSIC OF GREECE

With the breeze singing, the cloud is quietly
Staying in the clear sky.
The gravel path, the donkey cart,
and the orange blossoms
Are all dancing in the ancient garden.

Birds are flying around
From here to there.
Whilst kids are looking up into the sky
With their shining eyes.

Chinese parasol trees in late autumn have been
dyed into gold by the sun,
Their leaves fall through the open window
into the room.
There are colourful flowers on the sill.
A granny is sitting in a swaying chair,
Whose smiles makes the face fill with wrinkles.

< 34 >

PENCIL TREE

A child is walking in,
with his front teeth biting an apple.
A puppy is jumping over,
with granny's dress in its mouth.
The beautiful guitar music is out of another window,
travelling from one family to another.

< 35 >

THE AUTUMN

Hoary Stocks are blooming over the white wall.
Granny is sitting in the blue house,
Whilst children are singing at the toy room.
Following the breeze comes the waves of the Aegean Sea,
Making the birds keep chirping.

At the shady courtyard,
There are delicious wines
That are ready to drink.
The Aegean Sea welcomes everybody by opening
all the doors.
The sun is shining and turning the scene
into a fantastic painting.

< 36 >

Huaicun

< 37 >

THE CHILDREN

The sky and the spray are dancing at beach.
In the tidy room,
A group of children are springing to the book,
While nibbling the bread.

Their whisper can be heard now and then
from the seashore.
The warm breeze keeps blowing
Over the Aegean Sea into the clear hut.

The hall is full of sunlight.
The flowers are blooming,
The children frolicking, and
The butterflies flying around.
If listened carefully, it is Athena's music.

< 38 >

PENCIL TREE

The hut is in the fairy tale
Where a girl is declaiming the prayer.

The sky is azure, and
The sea blue.
Athena is dancing in the music.

< 39 >

THE PLEASURE

I see myself walking into the room full of art works.
The stars are dancing in the sky, and
The flowers growing in the field.
The breeze in autumn is fascinating
the moon by the window.

Suddenly, the pleasure fills my heart,
Just like the sunflowers blooming in the field.
My laughter can even be heard in the branches.
The leaves are green,
on top of which the dewdrops are dancing.

The blossoms
Are flourishing one by one.
The breeze gently holds up my dream,
Whilst the moon is squinting into the window.

It is just like me in childhood,
Who was rolling around in the moonlight.

< 40 >

THE MEMORY

It is the winding river
That attracts our
Attention.
It is the beautiful melody
That echoes in our
Mind.

It is not the dust
That covers the footsteps in the past.
It is not the snow
That conceals the road towards the future.
It is the gentle breeze
That writes down the poems and
Flips the pages.

The fantastic memory
Is the beautiful recall in my life.

< 41 >

THE DREAM

It is you

Who provide colours to the dream,

Making the whole world a beautiful paint.

When you are in spring,

The dream is green,

Making the field grassy, and

The earth buzzy.

When you are in summer,

The dream is azure,

Dying the ocean in blue

With your deep broad mind.

You are approaching

With hopes and ambitions.

< 42 >

PENCIL TREE

When you are in autumn,

The dream is golden.

The earth is decorated in yellow

By the mature grains.

You lead people into the season of harvest, and

Into the fields full of ripe crops.

When you are in winter,

The dream is white,

Resembling charming snowflakes.

You are as pretty as a fairy,

Magically ornamenting the world with white.

It is you

Who provide colours to the dream,

Making the life wonderful, and

the world beautiful.

< 43 >

THE SONG HIDING IN THE GARDEN

There is a song hiding in the garden

Where I planted a poplar

With Mum,

Watering and

Waiting for it to sprout every day.

< 44 >

PENCIL TREE

It is snowing,
My steps invisible, and
So are Mum's.
Where is the poplar?
Why can't I see the poplar planted by Mum and I?
My house seems to be a train,
Running on the track every day.

However,
I cannot bring the song in the garden,
The poplar planted by Mum and me,
And my childhood on the train.

Time is never going backward.
Only
A song between Mum and me
Is hiding in the garden.

< 45 >

CHASING UP THE SUNLIGHT

We are chasing up the sunlight,
And the fantastic future.

I shake hands with the sunlight,
Receiving its warm greeting, and
Watching its splendid colours.

Our mind is shining
Through the place where the sunlight is fond of.
Our imagination is flying
Around the universe where the sun is glowing.

I have seen the sparkling sunlight
In the bird's eyes,
Who spreads its wings in the wind and
Warbles happily.

< 46 >

PENCIL TREE

The laughter of the sunlight is heard by the cloud,
Who immediately turns into a joyful breeze.
The laughter of the sunlight is wafting in the forest,
Who instantly converts into the pleasant ocean.

When the sunlight is smiling,
We start to dream innocently, whilst
Wake up the stars and
And the flowers,
Making ourselves even more sincere and generous.

We are chasing up the sunlight, and
Lighting up our hope.

< 47 >

THE SPRING NEVER STOPS.

The spring never stops.

When I pass her,

She gradually turns into a white cloud.

Following the colourful spring, and

In the gentle breeze,

My happiness is full of each day of the spring

in London.

The spring never stops.

Magnolias are blooming.

How beautiful they are,

Like drops of water making the whole tree glitter!

When you watch her quietly,

She gazes at you emotionally.

The spring never stops.

When I fix my eyes on her,

She converts into the breeze at dusk.

I am in the beautiful white dress and

Flying up to the clouds with my minds.

< 48 >

The spring never stops.
She keeps growing in the breeze in April,
Just like the blooming flowers.

The spring never stops.
When I pass her,
She gradually turns into white clouds.

Huaicun

< 49 >

THE SECRET OF THE PENCIL TREE

I am hiding in a pencil tree,
With eyes opening widely.
I am wondering
How to make the beautiful tree grow up quickly, and
How to make the time pass promptly
So that the pencil tree can
deliver tasty fruits immediately.
This is the secret of the pencil tree.
A lot of stories are coming out pleasantly.
They are walking down from the pencil tree,
Passing the fields in spring,
Crossing the rivers in summer,
Travelling on the grasslands in autumn, and
Traversing the ocean in winter.
There are grown-up pencil trees everywhere.
There are dense pencil trees all over the world.

< 50 >

THE DANDELIONS

The earth is my mum,
With whose nutrients,
I am growing up
Joyfully
In the warm sunlight.

The wind blows me up
To fly all over the world.
Wherever I arrive, it is my home.

My mum and I,
Together with my siblings,
Are making the fields even more charming.

< 51 >

THE MORNING GLORY

Each morning glory seems to be a trumpet.
When the wind is blowing,
The flower is singing
With pleasure.

Look,
The red is marked,
The blue bright,
The purple simple, and
The white pure.

The busy bees are flying
In the morning glories,
Gladly singing and
Dancing.

< 52 >

LOVE FROM MUM

Love from Mum seems to be water
That I need every day.

Love from Mum seems to be food
That I have every day.

Love from Mum seems to be clouds
That I am watching every day.

Love from Mum seems to be air
That I cannot live without.

Love from Mum seems to be sunlight
That shines me all the time.

< 53 >

THE GRASS

Dressing
In green,
It starts quietly.

Swaying
In the sun,
It develops gradually.

Dancing
In the rain,
It grows up amazingly.

Hi, the grass,
It is you who makes me strong,
And cheers me up.

< 54 >

WISHES

I wish I could be a waterdrop
In the sea,
Staying in and
Never being evaporated.

I wish I could be a stone
In the gravel path,
Sticking to my friends and
Never making people stumble.

I wish I could be a well
In the field,
Providing water to
The thirsty people forever.

< 55 >

MY SCHOOLBAG

I pack
The breeze
And the sea
Into the schoolbag.

I pack
The flowers
And the morning sunlight
Into the schoolbag.

I pack
The voices of teachers
And laughter of classmates
Into the schoolbag.

I pack
Love from Mum
And dream of my own
Into the schoolbag.

< 56 >

< 57 >

THE AMAZING AUTUMN

When the dawn is standing by the window,
The night wakes up from the sleep.
Birds start chirping in the garden.
A chubby dew opens its eyes,
Rolling over to me
Along the wet path after rain.

When an autumn morning comes,
The sun runs out excitedly.
It swaggers through the city.
The Osmanthus tree is full of blossoms,
Like the shining eyes.
What a gorgeous Chinese ink painting it is!

The wind keeps singing,
As the notes wafting out from the piano.
It is a visitor from space
Who sings diligently.
All the dreams are bright.
The fantasies are travelling

< 58 >

PENCIL TREE

Through leaves by the colourful clouds.

When a flock of wild geese fly underneath the clouds,
They plant the seeds of fairy tales,
As well as the wishes of the children's and mine.

The dawn is approaching. It is in my city,
In the morning sunlight, and in everywhere.
How lucky I am!
I can imagine the autumn and the fairy tales
Under the sky where I am full of happiness.

Joys are flying over my heart and
Reach the castle in the fairy tale.
Picking up a ray of sunlight,
Seizing a string of laughter
I watch the pleasure spreading in the city.

< 59 >

I ONLY NEED
A SMALL PIECE OF LAND.

A ray of sunlight lands on the book,

And abounds my hand.

It is red, orange, yellow, green, blue, indigo, and violet,

Catching my eyes,

And tanning my skin.

My heart is flying in the sun,

Accompanied by the joyful laughter.

The sky is close to me,

Wearing the clothes of the clouds.

The earth puts on the green coat that belongs to the forest.

My lovely pencil tree embraces Aegean Sea

Emotionally,

Trying to turn the Greek stories to the fairy tales,

And hide into my favourite book of poems.

I have been attracted by the charming Aegean Sea,

People filling in the world of white and blue.

Is there anybody

Who is both fascinated and infatuated,

< 60 >

PENCIL TREE

And looking for the enchantment in the voice of Athena?
When birds fly across the lake,
The dream of childhood has been completed wakened.
Don't be shy.
Let's play house
In the blue space that has the same colour as countless
skies superimposing on numberless oceans,
In the lovely houses which are decorated with
red roofs and white walls,
And in the city of toys that is accidently lost by the angel.

My dear friends, please join us
To play house in the golden Athens
Till the sun hides itself into the sea.
Life is fully vibrant in autumn in Greece.
I wish I could be a tiny seed,
Who only needs a small piece of land.
Once planted, I will become a fairy tale of this season,
And keep blooming in the golden sun.

< 61 >

THE HOST IN THE FAIRY TALES

I am wondering whether I have grown up.

When turning around,

I find that the shadows of my childhood are followed,

Who keep singing gladly and walking right behind me.

But the recalls squeals,

"You have grown up already,

definitely and completely."

Am I? have I? I don't want to ask myself,

But to release some memory,

Memory of the happiness in childhood

Kept in the fairy tale box of my own for the autumn.

I stand in the river to whose falls the past approaches.

It is full of calm, innocence and happiness.

I can't help running

After the laughter of childhood to search.

The depth of the fairy tales is as inestimable as

The width of the sky.

But the fairy tales themselves have made me feel calm

In this autumn, and in the innocent smile of my daughter.

< 62 >

PENCIL TREE

Love of time
Is shining as the sun in the sky of mine.
A pretty girl leaves the sincere wishes
In my book,
Whispering to me:
Mum's heart seems to be a castle
full of happiness and hopes.
Wow, I am glad to say that I am as beautiful as before.
Nothing can make me feel even more pleasant
than my current imagination.

I add the wonderful fairy tales to the poems
And will take care of them for the rest of my life.
My castle is full of sunlight
And melodies this autumn.
I will be the hose in the fairy tales forever.

< 63 >

 PENCIL TREE

SUNLIGHT, A KIND OF LANGUAGE

Sunlight is a kind of language,
A language that can be listened to.

In the morning,
The sunlight comes out,
Talking to the green leaves
In a happy
And clear tone.
Whilst the flowers in the field
Are listening carefully.
Sunlight therefore greets to the flowers kindly.

In the clear sky
Walks the happy sunlight
To whom, on the ground,
We are joyfully listening.

< 64 >

HERE DEPARTS THE POETRY

My thoughts are dancing in the Osmanthus trees.
My clothes and hair are wetted by the dew,
And shoes and drawing board spotted by the mud.
However, I am full of exaltation.

When waking up in the morning,
I stretch my body with grass and breeze.
At that time, the ants are still sleeping,
But the butterflies have already started flying.

Whenever there are you, there are melodies.
In such a morning,
I write down these fantastic lines,
Snuffing up the fragrance of the flowers.

Osmanthus blossoms are sweet-melting,
the flowers blooming,
And to the ground the sunlight shining.
Here departs the poetry,
Making the mood as clear as the blue sky.

< 65 >

AT FAR END OF THE SKY

(1)

I am painting with a little bird,

A beautiful and cute creature.

When I draw a tree,

It lands on the branch gladly.

(2)

Listen, the melodious bird

Sings in the lawn.

The mischievous breeze

Flips my book deliberately.

(3)

The past, of the childhood, runs on my paper,

Sometimes dancing, sometimes whispering,

With joys and happiness.

On the grass in the sun,

The memories are strolling, singing, and dancing lightly.

< 66 >

(4)

My entire hope is to

Paint a picture for my childhood,

Or transform a bird to an elephant.

The endless imagination

Is hurtling on the grassland freely.

(5)

Look, the birds are flying

Over the top of the branches,

And at far end of the sky.

I wish I could fly up

To turn them into a poem instantly.

(6)

Just like the elephant swaying its long trunk,

The buddies who make us laugh

Are playing

On the grass in spring leisurely.

< 67 >

(7)

I am painting my childhood with rainbow colours

When a tiny cute ladybird

Is crawling across my picture

In its pretty spotty dress,

Leaving the red dots, black dots, and a string of red and black dots

forming an ellipsis amazingly.

(8)

The sunlight in March is playing on my hands.

The sun is napping on the sky at noon,

So do the breeze and the flowers.

Hi, the white butterfly,

Did you find a friend finally?

(9)

Ants are holding party in the lawn,

With the drumbeats everywhere.

The grass is swaying and dancing,

Making the night never as quiet as before.

I am slinking away.

I know tonight

There will be nobody falling asleep willingly.

< 68 >

PENCIL TREE

(10)

All the memories of childhood
Fly through the Osmanthus trees
And pass by the house of my parents.
The rose flavoured cake tastes sweet.
From the old family photos,
I find the childhood of my grandparents eventually.

(11)

My hair is dancing in the wind.
The sunlight lands on my face,
Creeps over my nose,
Lies at the corner of my mouth,
Leans to my ear,
And whispers secretly.

< 69 >

THE JOYS

The joys rush into my poems,
Just like a flower in spring
Dancing on top of the tree,
Flying over the leaves,
Running through the branches,
And landing onto my heart.
Its laughter makes the dream in spring even sweeter.

A river is flowing over there,
Quietly and poetically.
The joys conquer me promptly,
As fast as the wind flying across the sky,
As rapidly as the light travelling in the universe,
To kiss the flowers, the rivers and the birds.

< 70 >

PENCIL TREE

THE EYES

How the eyes are shining!
The same as flowers blooming.
One, two, three,
There are countless buds
Flourishing...

< 71 >

A STONE AT THE CORNER
OF THE STREET

There is an endless speech along the road.

My dear friend,

When we have fairy tales, the world is full of happiness.

The reason we use up all we have is because

we would like to search for the fairy tales.

We plant our childhood into the soil of poetry,

Leaving hope to the stone at the corner of the street.

A breeze passes by, singing a sweet song.

I believe this place is filled with fairy tales.

At the moment, a paragraph of the story is in my eyes,

Where it is frolicking like a cheerful fish.

< 72 >

PENCIL TREE

Huaiwun

< 73 >

THE PLACE WHERE FAIRY TALES INHABIT

It is the most magnificent place on the earth,
Where the angels were born.
They are as clear as the dewdrops at dawn.
They are as pleasant as a brook running down.

I am gazing here,
Breathing the fresh air,
Singing in a resounding voice,
And lying at a place that is the best choice.
I am trapped in the fantastic world of the children.

Do you think it is a painting?
    - Of course not.
It is a place where the fairy tales are inhabiting.
They are the fairies in the human world,
Who are flying all the time.

< 74 >

PENCIL TREE

Never deny

That they are delighted and sweet fairies,

That they are as fragrant as the grass in spring,

That they are the first and the last fairy tale in the world.

< 75 >

IS IT RAINING?

Bringing the fragrance of winter,
Someone walks into my studio,
 And falls to sleep,
Whom even the spring scares to wake up.

I hear my painting brush singing at night.
My child may climb up the stairs
To bring me a lovely toy
And a message from the spring.

The spatter of rain beating down against the window and roof,
I have never been so excited.
Neither has my studio
Been so quiet,
Silent and faint.

The spatter of rain beating down against the window and roof,
It is certainly drizzling.

< 76 >

Huaicun

< 77 >

A GARDEN FULL OF FOOTSTEPS

There is a big garden
Full of the footsteps I left when I was a child.
I planted a lot of poplars
And waited for their sprouting every day.

Shortly, it snowed.
I could not find the saplings.
My garden was completely covered
By the heavy snow.
Nothing was left to be seen.

Grandpa told me not to worry
as the snow seems to be the blanket,
And to be the warm house to
protect the saplings in the garden.
When the spring came, there must be miracles.
I then waited eagerly and proudly.

< 78 >

PENCIL TREE

Waiting for the surprises,

And waiting for the poplars.

At night, I dreamed about my poplars,

Who were sprouting, blooming,

And growing continuously.

< 79 >

EVERY SINGLE COLOUR SHOULD BE FLOURISHING.

Every single colour should be flourishing.
When the sun is shining,
Each of the colours is alive.
Please put the love gently on your palm
and come with me.

Let the brooks run into the sea,
The spindrifts dance in the field,
Dreams start to fly,
And love build up the brilliance of today.

The rain is running down with the fairy tales.
The happiness has transformed into drizzles.
When it is mizzling,
The fairy tales have become colourful.

< 80 >

< 81 >

A NIGHT AT MADRID

The drizzle lands on my face.
The colours of blue and white are full in my mind.
After travelling for a couple of days,
My world is filled with the clear blue and the crystal white.

Many people are still on the road.
The art keeps glittering.

From Barcelona to Madrid,
I cannot walk out of the forest.

The Alhambra,
Representing Arabic culture and decorated with Mosaic,
Displaying the amazing distribution
and gathering of the water,
Shows both the eastern quietude
and the western magnificence.

< 82 >

PENCIL TREE

At the red city,

The drizzle is talking to the Sierra Nevada far away.

The whole city is full of white walls and brown roofs,

Quiet and beautiful.

< 83 >

HYDRA

Joys twinkle in the field.
How clean and clear the sky is!
Birds fly over the sea.
Rushing out of the woods is the carriage.

The sunlight dwells on the shadowy trees.
Songs are wafting out of the house
that has red roof and white tiles.
In the far distance, speed boats are racing on water.
What a bright moonlight Hydra is under!

By the road, someone is whispering.
Flowers sway in the wind.
Below the orange tree, children are playing hide-and-seek.
The tall Chinese parasol tree is dancing
against the sea breeze.

< 84 >

PENCIL TREE

The overwhelming laughter burst out by the fishmen,
tourists and children
Is hovering above charming Hydra.

< 85 >

THE PRADO MUSEUM

There are friends of mine staying here,
Greco, Velázquez,
And Goya,
The most genius artists between 16th and 19th centuries,
As well as their remarkable paintings.

There are over five hundred artists I revere,
More than three thousand paintings I love,
 And more than one hundred halls I enjoy.

When walking in, I want to cry,
laugh and scream.
What an amazing time
that blends happiness and sadness!
I try to collect the scattered colours when feeling Greco.
I intend to embrace the golden crop
field made by Velázquez,
And fall asleep in 'the Saturn' completed by Goya.

< 86 >

PENCIL TREE

I am a Prado style now,
 Trying to take a sip of the Neptune's Fountain
To obtain the capacity to appreciate a masterpiece.
Suddenly a glare pierces my eyes
Followed by the splendid colours flying
over my forehead.

It is late at night now. But I find that I am still at Prado.

< 87 >

PLAZA DE ESPAÑA

Riding on the dream filled with colours of blue and white,
And following the rings of the bell,
I keep watching the birds flying in the sky,
As intently as the devout pilgrims
staring at the far distance.

I am standing at Plaza de España,
The whole world of mine has been lightened
by Don Quixote's attractive smiles.
When Sancho tells me the secrets of the words,
Time completely stops running in my thoughts.

Talking to Cervantes
Makes me quiver with excitement.
It seems that Plaza de España is melting
in the autumn sunlight.

< 88 >

PENCIL TREE

My heart starts to fly,
Whose feeling is the same as a child walking into the garden.
Dancing in the breeze,
Till the sun sets into my sleeve.
In Barcelona,
The sunlight is as bright as my smile in childhood.
Plump fruits are swaying on the tree.
In such a leisurely afternoon,
I am accompanied by Miró, Picasso and Dalí.

Picasso is declaiming to the sky,
Making the white houses in the field shiver.
The sunflowers all over the hill are flourishing,
Swinging with the leaves in the wind.

Walking in the colours created by Picasso,
I can feel his gaze mixed with tenderness and madness.
This piece of land is
Encircled by enthusiasm,
Decorated by the castles full of arts,
Shrouded by the dusk filled with quietness and flowers,
And run through by the classic river.

< 89 >

POEMS FOR CHILDREN

(1)

My heart is a tiny seed,

Hiding deep into the fairy tale.

When the laughter of children

Bursts out, and runs down the hill like the spring,

The seed starts to germinate,

Popping its head out of the fairy tale.

(2)

Here comes the bird,

Chirping.

Here runs the wind,

Rustling.

Here drifts in the rain,

Spattering.

Here jump out the children,

Bustling.

Here enters the teacher,

Smiling.

< 90 >

PENCIL TREE

(3)

The sunlight creeps into the window,
Shining into the room warmly.
The children sleep in their beds.
The teacher paces close to the door,
Gently and quietly.

Time moves from midday to the afternoon.
It is time for stories.
The teacher comes over again, and sits along the children's bed,
Softly and silently.

The sunlight is dancing
On the teacher's hair.

It is time to get up, children.
The teacher wakes up the children from their sweet dreams,
Slowly and kindly.
They get out of the bed,
With their hands rubbing their eyes.

< 91 >

PENCIL TREE

Shortly after,

The children sit in the classroom noiselessly,

Listening to the story told by the teacher.

It is a children's poem

About a baby growing up.

< 92 >

THE GRASS

You grow quietly, never coveting reputation.
You live in clusters,
Germinating
Silently.

You dress up the fields in the gorgeous green,
And provide beautiful lives to the world.

It is you
That encourage me
And cheer me up
On the journey of life.

< 93 >

STRENGTH OBTAINING FROM THE NORTH-WEST

As clear as the glass,

And as excited as a youngster travelling around

Are we, when sitting in the field

And listening to a kind of voices calmly.

When the wind blows

From the far distance,

I change into a colour

And a fate accordingly.

In the view of us at the same age,

The scene is as marvellous as troops marching.

The snow is light and heavy.

The sunlight is weak and strong.

The world is full of kindness.

Power from the desert

Lights up our spirits,

And helps us fly over the barren land.

< 94 >

 PENCIL TREE

Climbing over the mountain,
Walking across the ocean,
And standing under a pine tree,
I am thinking about
The expanse of the North-west
And the sultriness of the desert
Again and again.

Huaicun

< 95 >

A TREE FLOURISHING WITH SUNLIGHT

Time flies away quietly and silently.

The city is full of buttercups,
Spreading and flowering.
The Hanjiang River runs towards the sea,
Singing about the spring on the way.

The sound comes from the heart.

I keep painting,
trying to plant the colourful fairy tales
Onto my forehead,
And cultivating along my winkles.

I am a bird, flying over the forests,
And wheeling up in the sky.
My dear friend, please open the window.
The spring is approaching.
Let's invite the sunlight to come in.

< 96 >

PENCIL TREE

I try to use a fantastic brush
To carefully draw down
The mountains, brooks, forests and rivers.
I would like to describe the details of every single wave
coming in the morning,
And paint the splendid sceneries
on each day when it is fully of sunshine.

Writing is ingenuous, as normal as the soil.
Painting is marvellous, as magnificent as the ocean.

I am a little sapling,
Dancing in the whisper of the sunlight.
The birds standing on the branch compose of my verses.

In spring, I walk into the studio, speaking to the dyes.
In summer, I absorb in the computer,
chatting with the Chinese characters.
In autumn, I hold the dreams up.
In winter, I sleep in the world full of poems and paintings.

< 97 >

PENCIL TREE

How indescribable the beauty is!
What an unspeakable feeling it is!
I would like to change into a tree flourishing with sunlight
To decorate the fantastic and amazing world.

< 98 >

AUTUMN IN THE SOUTH

Summer has left, with its heart full of joys.
The clock of life keeps running, and never stops.

Autumn is approaching,
Whilst playing the flute loudly,
And dancing delightedly.

Golden ears of millet are heavy and weighty.
Orange leaves light and soft.
And red balloons swaying in bunches.

The heart is finally full of colours.

< 99 >

THE FRIENDSHIP

In such a flourishing season,
I am missing you deeply.
You seem to be the glamorous sunshine,
To warm me up.

Our friendship
Acts as a bee,
Gathering the pollens of love
And making the honey for love,
To create a better life.

When I succeed,
You congratulate me sincerely.
After I fail,
You soothe me cordially.

You are a star in the sky,
Illuminating the beautiful nights,
And weaving the prospective hopes,
To fill our life with sunlight.

< 100 >

DATING WITH THE SUN

I look through the sky and the clouds,
And find myself
Writing poems and drawing pictures.

Dewdrops stand on the lotus leave,
Glittering as crystals.
When the wind blows, they are rolling around.

In the breeze happily sing the birds,
Who are chirping while flying back to the forests,
When the sun sets.

We run in the field,
Looking for the spring fairy tales
And listening to the conversation among the grass on the ground.

< 101 >

FLYING

While the cloud is flying across the sky,

We are running on the earth,

Making the footsteps as loud as possible.

Look, what a wonderful world!

When hearing, the stars blink,

And the moon pouts.

Our hearts are as bright as the sunlight,

Dancing and soaring together.

< 102 >

YEARNINGS OF THE SEASONS

The greeting card I gave you when I was leaving
Seems to be a window of my heart,
Through which you can find out
My yearnings of the seasons.

In spring bloom the azaleas,
Among which we are laughing indulgently.

In summer smile the lotuses,
Under whose leaves we are frolicking freely.

 In autumn the maples turn red.
We pick up their leaves
And place them in a scarlet notebook.

In winter the snowflakes fall.
We stand on top of the mountain,
listening carefully to their rustling.

< 103 >

GRANDMA'S ADVICES

Grandma's advices

Are

Hiding

In the morning glow.

She smiles to me,

Or encourages me

To be a warrior of my life.

When the sun rises,

Grandma's advices

Shines in the rainbow colours,

Following which I run towards the sun.

< 104 >

PENCIL TREE

The splendid morning glow,
The helpful advice,
And the smile
From amicable Grandma
Are full of my childhood,
Making me as happy as
Dancing in the spring breeze,
And as delight as
Running in the sun.

Huaicun

< 105 >

A POEM WRITTEN
BY MY DAUGHTER

Riding a bicycle, and raising her head,
My daughter looks at me with her beautiful and watery eyes—
Mum,
The stars and the moon are running after me
In the sky.

Walking and skipping on the road,
My lovely daughter keeps talking—
Mum,
I am pushed to move forward by the trees, mountains and rivers
On the earth.

Sitting in the classroom straight,
My daughter holds the paint brush—
Mum,
The seed is germinating on the blackboard.

< 106 >

CHILDREN IN THE VILLAGE

Children in the village
Plant their days after school on the hill,
And give their sincere hearts to the earth and forests.
There definitely will be an ocean
Full of green
One day.

They climb over the fence
In the smile of their parents.
Ignoring the complaints from Grandma,
And filling the field with their prides.

Roving in the forest, they watch carefully,
Just like appreciating the full mark on their test paper.

< 107 >

MY DESIRE

My heart seems to be a seed

Deep hiding in the soil here.

The stories happened in my childhood

Are as fantastic as the blue sky

That bring the fondness of snow

In winter,

And cares of breeze

In summer.

I always have a deeply desire

That

My heart has already sprouted.

< 108 >

THE FRIENDSHIP

The friendship is like a green fruit,
Whose refuge is the wind.
As soon as they gaze at each other,
The green fruit turns ripened.

The friendship is a deep spring.
Please do not drink up.
Just sip when feeling sad
To forget all the worries in the world.

< 109 >

HOLDING MY TONGUE

I hold my tongue,
Allowing the tears
To run down into the sea full of books
And to talk to them.

I don't want to speak,
Leaving myself to surf in the books
And to chat with them.

I am running in the alley filled with stories,
Looking for Pippi Longstocking,
the Little Girl at the window,
Calabash Brothers, the Red Boy,
Smurfs and the Flower Child Lunlun.

< 110 >

A SONG IN MY HEART

There is a song
That is the one in my heart.

It is jumping,
Dancing,
And exciting.

One day,
I will sing it out
With my sweet voice.

< 111 >

HIDE-AND-SEEK

Stars are blinking.

The moon is laughing.

I am looking for the spring in your eyes

And searching for the song in your smile.

< 112 >

THE DRIZZLE IN SPRING

The world,
Decorating with green,
Soaks in the drizzle.
The world is full of poetry,
Talking about
The feeling of the spring.

< 113 >

A GREEN DREAM

The unripen fruits
Are hanging on the tree,
Which the naughty child
Is longing for.
He tries his best,
But it is too far to reach.
Without getting even one,
The child feels so sad.
After a gentle breeze,
He luckily
Finds an unmatured orange.
Though
It is not the one he expects,
He will still keep it in his memory.

< 114 >

PENCIL TREE

THE TEACHER

Lots of writings and drawings
Are done by you on the blackboard.
The colourful bubbles
Are flying up and down in the school playground.

An endless story is being written
In the teaching plan on the desk.
Many children are climbing up
The ladder of success.

From the hot summer to the cold winter,
And year after year,
You kindly gaze at the students in the class
And encourage them
To endeavour and to fight.

You believe
That
No pains today,
No gains tomorrow.

< 115 >

SPRING IS COMING
OUT OF MY POETRY

(1)

The rain in spring is drizzling
And spattering.
The breeze is flying over my notebook,
Whilst a bird is standing on the purlin.

At the moment, the grasses in the deep mud wake up.
They move across the hill, over the stones, through the soil,
And finally out of the surface. They look around
And try their best to grow as tall as to embrace the spring.

The breeze is approaching. They again raise up their hands
To hold the rain,
And walk delightedly on the ground.

< 116 >

PENCIL TREE

(2)

The sunlight is running on my palm

And never stops.

Lots of people are still looking for the spring.

When birds are warbling in the peach trees,

The vigorous vines are crawling in and out of the bridge.

(3)

There must be poetry in spring, growing.

Anyone passing here is a poet.

Spring is the lover of the poetry who

falls in love with spring at the first glance.

We are all poems passing the spring.

There are fruits in spring,

Who are full of the trees in the field.

In the warm sunlight,

Spring stands gracefully, and waits

For the poetry blooming.

< 117 >

(4)

Please open the door, allowing the sunlight to come in

And filling the room with joys.

Please leave the poetry with spring,

As spring is finally coming out of my poetry.

< 118 >

A DREAM IN THE MORNING

An elephant sits on one of the dewdrops
In the morning,
Holding another in its arms.

Frogs croak continuously,
Accompanying
The sound of reading wafting out from the class.

< 119 >

THE DREAM

My dream is to incarnate the sea,

Whom the coconut trees and the seaweed

Can absorb water from.

In such a way,

My wish to become the sea can be shown to others.

My joys seem to be the sun,

Bringing the lights and heat to people,

And helping the kids,

who are singing the songs for spring,

Grow up in the warm breeze.

< 120 >

SECRETS IN STAR HEART, ONE OF TWENTY-EIGHT ANCIENT CHINESE LUNAR MANSIONS

Every sentence here
Is sensitive and compact.
As soon as finding a space to squeeze in,
I can wander around quietly
And think about the secrets in Star Heart.

It is only when the sun sets
That I am able to
Write down my concerns
In the diary
And tell privately about
The secrets in Star Heart.

< 121 >

SLOWLY GROWING UP

Mum's hope
Is extending
On the child's innocent face.

Mum's desire
Is creeping
Along the child's skinny ankle.

Mum's dream
Is waiting
In the child's joyful laughter.

Growing up slowly and gradually.

< 122 >

THE WHITE MEMORY

It is the meandering river
That is knocking on
My heart.

It is the faraway singing
That is echoing in
My head.

Though not the dust,
It can cover the footsteps in the past.

Though not the snow,
It can inundate the road towards the future.

It is the warm breeze
That gradually releases
The memory of the childhood.

Such white memory
Is the gentlest part in my life.

< 123 >

ANSWER TO MY FRIEND

It is I who left my heart in the valley
During the travelling.
Years later, the heart turned to a snow lotus,
As clear as a crystal.

It is I who glided across the childhood
In the warm eyes,
Stamping the splendid scenery
On the fresh memory.

It is I who walked along the seashore on bare feet,
Carefully fiddling
The rainbow coloured shells,
But afraid to keep.

The more the days, the more the moods.
The more the moods, the more the tales.
It is I who put the stories occurred in childhood
Under the beach.

< 124 >

PENCIL TREE

When the memory is soaked by the rain,
When the season is driven by the breeze,
The only person strolling in the fairy tales
Is me.

< 125 >

THE GIRL WHO
WRITES AND DRAWS

Young people's expectations are ready to be written down.

Stars acknowledge

That my footsteps are left by the lake on a summer night.

The moon is aware

That I save the dreams in winter to recall in spring.

I have planted a seed named Poetry

In the field that is not too fertile.

I spend my whole youth

In waiting.

I am full of emotions

When watering.

I don't know whether the seed I planted

Will finally grow up.

Nor will I know if

The leaves are green,

The branches are strong,

Or the tree is blooming and full of fruits.

< 126 >

But I understand

That I will possess another kind of beauty

In my life

Even though I can harvest nothing after

Waiting quietly and

Watering industriously.

< 127 >

THE BREEZE

Listen! When the breeze
Is flying over my heart,
I am
Intoxicated.

Look! When the breeze
Is passing by me,
I am
Pleased.

Dream! When the breeze
Is drifting through my thoughts,
The scenery is
Splendid.

The breeze flying over,
The breeze passing by,
And the breeze drifting through,
Make my heart
Float
In the glorious world.

< 128 >

AN OASIS IN THE HEART

I keep looking for

The secret oasis in my heart.

From dust till dawn,

From spring to autumn,

Over the Poplar trees standing on the hill in North,

Among Japanese Banana trees locating at the village in South,

And in the alternation of the sun and moon,

Time has transformed the days into

Spring, summer, autumn and winter,

All of whom are subsequently divided into different seasons.

Many years later,

We are not children any more.

But there are lots of footsteps, either deep or shallow,

Left on the way towards growing up.

< 129 >

THE SUMMER

When the trees complete their process of sprouting,

Coming while carrying

The buds,

The birds escape to the forests,

And start

Singing about their beautiful home.

The path in the sun

Is quietly waiting

For the happy butterflies and the galloping horses.

At the very moment,

The summer

Is approaching

From the wet lane in the south.

< 130 >

PENCIL TREE

< 131 >

PENCIL TREE

I LOVE THIS PLACE

It is drizzling in my city.
I am reading Andersen's Fairy Tales by the fireplace,
And listening to the spatter of rain on the window.

I love this place.
The wind is whistling when flying over the window.
Tall and short trees keep whispering in the courtyard.
Blooming camellias are gracefully swaying,
Birds chirping with glee.

I love this place.
The sun is shining through my window,
Puppy napping on the carpet,
Kitten grunting by the heater,
Birds still warbling on the tree.

< 132 >

PENCIL TREE

I love this place,

Writing and painting at here every day.

I love this place. These are the reasons why.

It is in the depth of winter, but

The pine trees and grass

Are still dressing in green, looking so pretty.

< 133 >

TO SPENDING MY WHOLE
LIFE TAKING CARE OF YOU

I seem to be a seed,

Whose hands are holding all the rainbow colours—

Red, Orange, Yellow, Green, Blue, Indigo and Violet.

The sunlight shines into my eyes,

Walking past my heart

And flying in the laughter.

The sky borrows a coat from the cloud.

The earth is wearing the green gown gifted by the forest.

I turn the Greek stories into fairy tales,

And hide them into my favourite poems.

When three birds fly over the clear water,

The panoramic picture of my childhood is completely spread out.

< 134 >

PENCIL TREE

Don't worry.
Just let me walk, play games and hide-and-seek
In the dense forest.
Allow me to look for the stories happened in childhood
Along the coast from dawn till dusk.

I seem to be a seed,
Who will root, germinate, bloom and fruit.
I would like to transform to a fairy tale,
And to spend the whole life taking care of you.

< 135 >

LISTENING

When birds fly back home and start singing,
I sit in front of the canvas, snuggling up to Granny
And reading about her smile,
Who at the same time is talking
about what happened in my childhood.
Such life is as normal as the clear sky,
but full of happiness.

Granny believes that everything will finally
return to the nature.
Shall we open doors and windows,
Listen to the sound of nature together,
And chat with the flowers in the garden?
When whispering to the ants in the lawn,
I find out that they will cry, laugh, delight,
And frolic in the autumn breeze.

When the wind is quietly passing by,
Granny is laughing aloud.

< 136 >

PENCIL TREE

She sits in the Mahogany chair decorated with pearl shells,
Recalling her early life and the poems about her childhood.
All the memories are rooting and germinating.

Keep listening.
Listen to myself, to the nature, and to the world.
Listen to Granny, and to the life.

Ants start playing music after returning home.
I am snuggling up to Granny
To read our Peter Rabbit.

Just leave the stars hanging in the sky.
Just ask the earth to come back.
Please come over.
Let's listen to the sound of nature together.
Turning off the music and closing the book,
I will listen carefully with the breeze.

Shall we listen to the seed of a star germinating?

< 137 >

SUMMER COMES OVER AFTER GRANNY.

It is seven o'clock in the morning,

outdoor temperature eleven degree Celsius.

Summer is quietly arriving in Britain when people are sleeping,

It comes over after Granny.

When the sun is shining,

the whole world decorated in green,

Life rests in placidity and promise.

The fragrance of summer is everywhere.

Shall we put down all the cares,

And enjoy ourselves on the summer morning

When the birds are happily warbling?

While passing here every day,

I am as joyful as a child.

Gentle breezes,

Light drizzles,

Bright sunshine,

And heavy showers

Surprisingly happen in turn in the British summer.

< 138 >

PENCIL TREE

No matter it is sunny or rainy,
I will continue my passion…

Summer comes over after Granny.
When traveling with Granny,
We will take along the easel, the paints, and the sketchbook,
As well as our zest and romance.

Clouds are floating in the sky,
Who are left behind
When we keep driving on.
Granny believes that the clouds can be easily reached
If we turn around right now.
The British summer comes over after Granny.
Its fragrance is everywhere.

< 139 >

This book is the result of a co-publication agreement between Ms Zhang Huaicun and Paths International Ltd (UK)

Title: Pencil Tree
Author: Zhang Huaicun
Hardback ISBN: 978-1-84464-700-2
Paperback ISBN: 978-1-84464-701-9
Ebook ISBN: 978-1-84464-702-6
Copyright © 2022 by Young Paths Childrens Books LTD.

Young Paths Childrens Books LTD.
Paths International Ltd
www.pathsinternational.com
Published in United Kingdom